Princess

ANGELICA

Part-Time Lion Trainer

Princess
ANGELICA
Part-Time Lion Trainer

Monique Polak

Illustrated by **Jane Heinrichs**

orca Echoes

ORCA BOOK PUBLISHERS

Library and Archives Canada Cataloguing in Publication

Polak, Monique, author
Princess Angelica, part-time lion trainer / Monique Polak; illustrated by Jane Heinrichs.
(Orca echoes)

Issued in print and electronic formats.
ISBN 978-1-4598-1547-6 (softcover).—ISBN 978-1-4598-1548-3 (PDF).—
ISBN 978-1-4598-1549-0 (EPUB)

I. Heinrichs, Jane, 1982–, illustrator II. Title. III. Series: Orca echoes

PS8631.O43P76 2019   jC813'.6   C2018-904869-7
                    C2018-904870-0

Simultaneously published in Canada and the United States in 2019
Library of Congress Control Number: 2018954077

Summary: In this illustrated early chapter book, Angelica allows a
new friend to believe she is a part-time lion trainer.

Orca Book Publishers gratefully acknowledges the support for its publishing
programs provided by the following agencies: the Government of Canada,
the Canada Council for the Arts and the Province of British Columbia through
the BC Arts Council and the Book Publishing Tax Credit.

Edited by Liz Kemp
Cover artwork and interior illustrations by Jane Heinrichs
Author photo by John Fredericks

ORCA BOOK PUBLISHERS
orcabook.com

Printed and bound in Canada.

22 21 20 19 • 4 3 2 1

*For my pal Jonah Kinsella,
who loves to read*

Chapter One

"Where's Mwezi? Do you think she escaped?" Joon asks.

Joon and I are standing outside the giant enclosure at the animal rescue center where Mwezi lives.

I scan the grass and the small hill at the back of the enclosure. I spot a golden, tasseled tail under a low bush. A tassel is like a messy knot. Lions are the only cats with tasseled tails. "There she is," I tell Joon, pointing to the bush.

The tail thumps.

"I think she recognizes your voice," Joon says.

"And also my smell. I've known Mwezi longer than I've known you," I tell Joon.

Joon and I met at sleepaway camp. When I told her and the girls in our bunk that I was a princess, they believed me. Things got complicated when they learned I wasn't really royalty. Luckily, they forgave me. It helped that my storytelling got us out of a sticky situation.

I've known Mwezi all my life. I've even helped feed her. My parents are on the board of directors for the animal rescue center. I've been coming here since I was a baby in a Snugli.

Mwezi came to live at the center because one of her hind legs doesn't work right. The injury happened years ago when Mwezi lived in Tanzania, and her leg got caught in a wire snare trap. At the time, Ms. Jessup, who is now the director of the center, was in Africa learning how to help injured lions. Ms. Jessup is a certified big-cat keeper. When she returned to Canada, she brought Mwezi with her.

These days Mwezi spends most of her time napping, which is normal for a lion. When it's hot outside, like it is today, she finds herself a shady spot and settles in.

"I wish there was some way to make her come over to see us," Joon says.

"I know a trick to get Mwezi's attention," I tell Joon. Lions can hear noises from a mile away. So I blow hard on the bars on the outside of Mwezi's enclosure. In the distance I see Mwezi's golden ears turn in our direction.

Then Mwezi gets up from her spot and comes bounding over to us.

"Wow!" Joon says when Mwezi rubs her cheek against the bars.

"You could get a job as a lion tamer," Joon says. "You could wear a sparkly tuxedo."

"Sparkly clothes are not my style," I tell Joon. "And I'd never want to be a lion *tamer*. But I would like to be a lion *trainer* or a *big-cat keeper* like Ms. Jessup."

"I have never heard of either of those jobs before," Joon says.

"People don't use the term *lion tamer* much anymore. Lion *trainers* don't just teach lions to do tricks, they teach people how to treat lions. Big-cat keepers like Ms. Jessup educate the public too. They also protect lions and tigers in captivity."

When Mwezi opens her mouth, Joon jumps several feet back. Now Mwezi roars.

Lionesses do not roar as loudly as lions do, but Mwezi's roar is loud enough that the porcupine in the next enclosure scuttles off to the rocky crevice where he lives.

I can't help thinking that Mwezi is agreeing with what I just told Joon. Mwezi does not want to be *tamed*. But I don't think she minds being *trained*. I also think she'd like people to learn more about lions.

Joon and I brought sandwiches for lunch. Our parents gave us money to buy ice cream in the cafeteria.

The cafeteria is in the main building where the offices are. On our way in, we see Ms. Jessup. "Why, Angelica!" she says. "It's lovely to see you here today."

I feel proud that someone as important as Ms. Jessup knows my name.

I introduce Joon.

"I really like your animal rescue center," Joon tells Ms. Jessup. "But your cafeteria needs to have more flavors of ice cream. A lot of people think vanilla is boring."

"Thanks for your suggestion, Joon," Ms. Jessup says. She turns back to me. "Angelica, I'm setting up the conference room for a meeting. If you don't mind, could you carry in a chair for me?"

"It would be an honor," I tell her.

Ms. Jessup points to a wooden chair in the hallway and to the conference room down the hall. The chair is not heavy. I pick it up and head down the hall. Joon is giving Ms. Jessup more suggestions. Joon thinks the main building needs air-conditioning.

A boy wearing a gray baseball cap is walking toward me. He looks like he is about my age.

The boy eyes the chair I am carrying. "Hey," he says to me, "are you a lion trainer?"

"Uh…" I am about to say no. Maybe the boy has mistaken me for a lion trainer because of the chair I am carrying. He has probably seen pictures of old-fashioned circuses, where lion *tamers* waved chairs in front of lions.

"I'm doing research about kids with unusual jobs," the boy says. "It's for my school newspaper."

"But school doesn't start for another month," I say.

"I'm writing my article in advance. It's for the first edition," he says.

I could explain the difference between tamers, trainers and big-cat keepers.

I could tell the boy he has made a mistake.

But I don't.

Instead I say, "It's a pleasure to meet you. I'm Jelly, the new part-time lion trainer. I'd be happy to answer your questions."

Chapter Two

The boy's name is Leopold. He just moved to the neighborhood, and he lives close enough to the animal rescue center that he can walk over by himself. Leopold wants me to show him the way to the cafeteria.

Leopold has many questions about lions. Luckily, I have most of the answers. After all, I'm a part-time lion trainer, aren't I?

Leopold opens his notebook and takes out his pen. "Why doesn't Mwezi have a mane?" he asks.

"Because she's a lioness. Only male lions have manes."

"How much does Mwezi weigh?" Leopold wants to know.

"About four hundred pounds. A male lion weighs closer to five hundred pounds."

"What kind of tricks have you trained Mwezi to do?"

"All kinds!"

Joon waves when she sees us. Leopold follows me to the table where Joon is sitting.

I wink at Joon, trying to signal her that if Leopold mentions lion training, she should play along. But Joon does not understand my signal. "Is something wrong with your eye, Jelly?" she asks.

I shake my head hard.

Joon still doesn't get it.

"Joon," I say, "this is Leopold. Leopold, this is my friend Joon. We were bunkmates at sleepaway camp. Joon likes my stories." I shoot her a sharp look when I say the word *stories*.

"Oh, Jelly tells the best stories. At camp she told us she was a pr—"

I am about to raise my palm in the air to stop Joon, but I don't need to. That's because Leopold interrupts her. "A part-time lion trainer must have a lot of great stories," he says.

"Part-time lion trainer?" Joon says. Thank goodness she does not laugh.

"That's right," I say quickly. "I didn't have a chance to tell you yet, Joon. But Ms. Jessup offered me this great job. It's for the rest of the summer, and then once school starts, I'll be working on Saturday mornings."

I hope Joon won't spoil my fun.

"Congratulations!" she says.

That's when I realize Joon believes my story too.

I tell Joon that Leopold is writing a story about kids with unusual jobs for his school newspaper, and that he wants to interview me.

But Joon is more interested in the turkey sandwich Leopold has brought for lunch. She's impressed that there are slices of avocado in the sandwich. "Turkey and avocado go well together," she notes.

"Joon loves talking about food," I tell Leopold.

"Jelly loves talking about lions," Joon says.

Leopold takes a bite of his sandwich. "So what sorts of tricks have you been teaching Mwezi?" he asks.

"Have you heard of horse whisperers?" Joon asks Leopold. "They are people with a gift for communicating with horses. Jelly is a lion whisperer. When she blows on the bars of Mwezi's enclosure, Mwezi comes over and rubs her cheek against the bars."

"That's not all," I say. "Joon hasn't seen half of the tricks I've taught Mwezi."

"I haven't?" Joon says.

I get the tingly feeling that comes when I start inventing a story. "I can get Mwezi to lie on her back so I can scratch her tummy," I tell them.

"Wow!" Joon says.

"Isn't that dangerous?" Leopold asks.

"It could be if someone else tried it," I say. "Besides, that's what the chair

15

is for. I keep it handy when I'm inside the enclosure. If I thought Mwezi might be about to attack me—not to worry, because that has never happened—I'd hold the chair between us, and Mwezi would attack the chair instead. That's why in old-fashioned circuses, the lion trainer always carried a chair—and a whip."

Leopold looks under the table. "Do you have a whip?"

"No way," I tell him. "I believe in *positive reinforcement training*."

Leopold wipes the bread crumbs from his chin and opens his notebook to a fresh page. "That's a lot of big words. What do they mean?"

Our next-door neighbor has a dog, so I know all about positive reinforcement training. "It means that instead of

punishing bad behavior, the dog tr—the lion trainer rewards positive behavior. So when Mwezi lets me scratch her tummy, I give her one of these." I fish a meatball out of my lunch bag. My mom made me a meatball sub for lunch, but I couldn't finish all of it. "Mwezi loves meatballs."

"With or without tomato sauce?" Joon asks.

"Without."

Now, because I am really getting into my story, I come up with even more tricks to tell Leopold and Joon about. "I've trained Mwezi to give me a paw. I've trained her to jump through a hoop. For two meatballs, Mwezi even lets me ride on her back."

Joon's jaw falls open.

Leopold has another question. "Have you ever put your head in Mwezi's mouth?"

"Of course!" I say. "In fact, I do it all the time!"

Chapter Three

Leopold and Joon want to see me put my head in Mwezi's mouth.

"It isn't the best day for it," I tell them. "Mwezi has a toothache."

"I didn't know lions could get toothaches," Joon says.

Leopold watches my face. "Are you sure that isn't an excuse?" he asks.

"Of course it's not an excuse! Putting my head in Mwezi's mouth is one of my favorite tricks. Did you know that when a lion opens its mouth, the space inside is bigger than the length of a human head? That's why old-fashioned lion tamers invented the trick in the first place."

I try to distract Leopold with lion facts. Maybe then he'll stop asking me to show him the trick. "Did you know that a lion's back teeth are called *carnassials*?"

"You use a lot of big words," Leopold says. "How many *s*'s are there in *carnassials*?"

"Three *s*'s, including the one at the end," I tell him.

"Jelly always uses big words when she talks about lions," Joon chimes in.

"Carnassials work like scissors," I add. "They are the teeth that help lions chew meat. Did you know that lions' claws are *retractable*?" I'll have to explain that word too. "All cats, even house cats, have retractable claws. Retractable means a cat or a lion can pull in his claws and extend them when he needs to. Retractable claws prevent injury when cats or lions are playing. I bet you didn't know that lions love to play. Most animals do."

"*I* love to play," Joon says.

Leopold drums his fingers on the cafeteria table. "So are you going to show us how you put your head in Mwezi's mouth or not?"

My lion facts are not enough to distract Leopold. Lions use their claws when they have to. I tell stories when I need to. I lean back in my chair. "Did I ever tell you about the time I lived in Africa?" I ask Joon and Leopold.

"You never told me!" Joon says.

"You only met me an hour ago, so when exactly would you have told me?" Leopold asks.

I ignore Leopold's question. Besides, I can feel a new story taking shape in my brain. "My parents and I lived in northern Tanzania, near the Serengeti Plain." I know about the Serengeti because I've read about it in books and heard Ms. Jessup talk about it. "That was when I first got interested in lions. We saw them all the time." When I look outside, I spot a pigeon on the windowsill. "Lions on the Serengeti Plain—they're like pigeons in Canada. You see them everywhere all the time!"

"I see pigeons so often I don't even notice them," Joon says.

"I always noticed lions when we lived in Africa," I tell her.

Leopold clicks on his pen. "Why did you move to Africa in the first place?" he asks.

"Because...well..." I decide to work some truth into my story. It's a trick that has worked for me before. "Because my parents are lawyers. Mostly they handle human rights cases, but we moved to Africa so they could fight for lions' rights. In Africa, poachers hunt lions so they can sell their teeth, skins and claws. My parents took poachers to court. Because we lived so close to the Serengeti, I made friends with many of the lions my parents helped save. Including Mwezi."

"You never told me that!" Joon says.

"Mwezi's hind leg was caught in a poacher's wire snare trap. My dad was driving the Jeep and I was looking out the window with my binoculars when I spotted her. Poor Mwezi." My voice gets sad. After all, the part of the story about Mwezi's leg getting caught in the trap is true. I may not have been there to see it, but I've certainly imagined it.

"Are you the one who got her out of the trap?" Joon asks. She knows I like fixing stuff.

"Of course!" I can feel my story starting to speed up. My voice speeds up too. "My dad used a dart gun to tranquilize Mwezi. But no matter how hard he tried, he couldn't get her leg loose. There was no wire cutter in the Jeep. But I remembered that my mom kept her fingernail clippers in the glove compartment. So I used them!"

"Wow!" Joon says. "You're amazing, Jelly."

I throw back my shoulders. I feel as proud as if I really did free Mwezi from that trap.

Leopold rolls his eyes. "Fingernail clippers?" he says. "If you saved her, why did she have to come to an animal rescue center?"

I am good at answering tough questions. Besides, I know another lion fact that is about to come in handy.

"Did you know that lionesses can run at a speed of up to fifty miles an hour? After Mwezi recovered, we timed her, and she could only run ten miles an hour. That's not fast enough for a lioness to survive on the Serengeti Plain. Thank goodness my parents knew Ms. Jessup. She found an enclosure for Mwezi here."

Chapter Four

Leopold and Joon want to hear more
stories about Mwezi.

Leopold suggests we sit on the bench
outside Mwezi's enclosure.

Mwezi is lying in the sunshine at the
back of her pen.

"You should show Leopold your
trick for getting Mwezi to come over,"
Joon says. She slides to the end of the

bench, making room for Leopold and me. I am about to tell Joon and Leopold that I think it is best to let Mwezi rest so she can recover from her toothache when there is a loud *thunk*.

Joon is lying flat on her back beside the bench. Her legs are up in the air like an upside-down table.

I help Joon to her feet.

She shakes some dry leaves from her hair. "I don't know what happened," she says.

"Here!" Leopold says. "Let me try!"

There is something wrong with the bench, because Leopold slides off too. He lands with a *thunk* in the same spot.

"This bench is dangerous," Joon says. "We should tell Hilda about it."

Hilda is the custodian.

Joon points across the way to the porcupine's enclosure. "Isn't that Hilda over there?"

Hilda comes over when we call her. "Hmm," she says as she kneels down to examine the bench. "I don't think this bench can be fixed. I will tell Ms. Jessup to order a new one. I will also need to make a sign warning people not to sit here. While I am gone, could you three make sure no one uses this bench?"

Joon and Leopold sit on the ground, a safe distance from the bench. I decide to take a better look.

Leopold shakes his head when he sees what I am up to. "Hilda told us to make sure no one uses the bench," he says.

"I am not *using* the bench," I tell him. "I am *inspecting* it."

"Did I mention Jelly is good at fixing things?" Joon asks Leopold.

"Hilda said the bench cannot be fixed," Leopold says.

"No," I correct him, "Hilda said that she did not *think* the bench could be fixed. I have a different opinion."

It does not take me long to figure out the problem. One of the bench's wooden legs is cracked. If I could find an object about the height of one of the legs, I might be able to prop up the bench. If my repair was solid, this old bench would be safe to use until the new one arrives.

I look up at the sky. Sometimes ideas come to me when I am gazing at the clouds. But today the sky is perfectly blue. There are no clouds to inspire me.

Sometimes I get ideas when I am moving. So instead of staying in a squat on the ground, studying the problem, I get up and stretch my arms.

"What in the world are you doing now?" Leopold asks.

"Thinking," I tell him.

"I have never seen anybody think while they are stretching," Leopold says.

I walk to the oak tree that grows outside Mwezi's enclosure and press the sole of my foot against the tree's thick trunk.

That's when I notice the tin pail. It is the sort of pail animal keepers use to bring food to the animals at the center. Someone must have forgotten the pail here. I take it back to the bench. It is about the same height as the legs of the bench.

I flip the pail over. That way the wider end will be on the ground, making the bench more solid. I wedge the pail into place. It fits! I push on the other three legs and on the pail to make sure the bench is solid.

"Don't!" Leopold shouts when he sees me sit down on the bench.

"Don't what?" I ask him. I wave from the bench. It does not wobble, and I do not slide off.

"I told you Jelly was good at fixing things!" Joon tells Leopold.

"I see that," Leopold says. "Jelly, call Mwezi over. Then you can show us how you put your head in her mouth!"

Chapter Five

"Today's not a good day for me to put my head in Mwezi's mouth," I tell Leopold. The three of us are sitting on the newly fixed bench. "You know, Mwezi's toothache. Poor thing."

But I can show Leopold my trick for getting Mwezi to come over. I get up from the bench and blow hard against the bars of the enclosure. In the distance we can see Mwezi's golden ears turn up, but she does not come bounding over.

Joon sighs. "It usually works," she tells Leopold.

"Maybe Mwezi is tired. Toothaches can tire a lioness out," I say.

Joon raises one finger in the air. "There's something I've been wondering about, Jelly. And maybe Leopold will want to use the answer in his article. When did you first know you wanted to become a lion trainer?"

"That is a good question," Leopold says.

"I knew the minute I found Mwezi trapped in the snare. It might have been the way she looked at me with those orange eyes of hers. Like we were already friends."

"Is that the way I look at you?" Joon asks.

"Exactly. Except that your eyes aren't orange."

This conversation reminds me of another interesting thing about lions. "The fact that Mwezi's eyes were orange helped us figure out her age. When female lion cubs are born, their eyes are bluish-gray, but when the cubs are two to three years old, their eyes turn orange," I tell Joon and Leopold.

"You sure know a lot about lions," Leopold says.

I am so pleased by the compliment, I nearly roar. "That's because in today's world, lion trainers don't just teach lions to do tricks. Another important part of a lion trainer's job is teaching people about lions—and about what we can do to protect lions who live in the wild and in refuge centers. Big-cat keepers like Ms. Jessup do that too."

"So you're a lion trainer and a people teacher," Joon says.

"Exactly."

"A group of lions is called a pride," Leopold says. I guess I'm not the only one who knows lion facts—although that one is pretty basic.

"Correct," I say. "But do you know who in the pride hunts for food?" I ask Leopold.

"I bet it's the male," he says.

"Wrong!" I call out. "It's the lioness!"

"How interesting," Joon says.

At that moment Hilda marches over. She is carrying a long sheet of plywood. On it she has written the words:

Hilda drops the sign to the ground when she spots us. "What are you three doing?" she asks. "I asked you to keep people from sitting on that broken bench."

"Jelly fixed it," Leopold tells her.

"She is good at fixing things," Joon adds.

Hilda makes a harrumphing sound. "Get off that bench on the double so I can check if it is safe!"

We scramble off the bench. When Hilda looks at the bench, she harrumphs again. At first I think she has found a new problem. But then she looks up at me and says, "Nice job, Jelly!"

Hilda walks over to the enclosure. "Good afternoon, Mwezi!" she calls out.

"Mwezi is resting in the sun," Joon tells Hilda. "She has a toothache."

Hilda harrumphs for the third time. "A toothache?" she says. "That's odd. Nobody told me anything about that."

Hilda's radio goes off. We hear Ms. Jessup's voice crackling on the other end of the line. She needs Hilda to report to the main building.

Leopold scrunches up his eyes as he looks at me. "Are you *sure* Mwezi has a toothache? Hilda seemed surprised to hear about it."

"Of course I'm sure. Besides, I'm the part-time lion trainer. Not Hilda!"

Leopold scrunches up his eyes again. "Maybe, Jelly, you're *afraid* to put your head in Mwezi's mouth."

"Of course I'm not afraid!"

That is when I realize it is time to come up with another story. And it had better be a good one! Otherwise, I may really have to put my head in Mwezi's mouth. And though Mwezi likes me, there is always a chance that she could eat me. Not that she has ever harmed a human being. But Mwezi is a lioness after all—so I'd rather not put my head in her mouth.

"Did I ever tell you about Mwezi's airplane ride to Canada?" I ask Leopold and Joon.

"Did she travel in cargo—in the belly of the airplane?" Joon asks.

"Of course not! Mwezi had her own seat," I say. "Two seats, in fact!"

Chapter Six

Sometimes I plan my stories in advance, like when I tricked my best friend, Maddie, into thinking there was an elevator in my house. Other times, I can feel a story growing in my head.

That's what happens with my story about Mwezi's airplane ride.

"The seat belt was a bit of a problem," I tell Joon and Leopold. "Airplane seat belts are not designed for four-hundred-pound lionesses."

Joon claps her hands. "I bet you found a way to fix that problem!"

"As a matter of fact, I did. I borrowed my dad's belt. His pants were loose without it, but he didn't mind. And when I attached my dad's belt to the seat belt, and it still wasn't big enough for Mwezi, I went to the flight deck and asked the pilot if I could borrow his belt too."

Leopold scrunches up his eyes again. "Passengers are not allowed on the flight deck," he says.

"The plane was still on the ground, and the door to the flight deck was open. The pilot was really nice about it. He even asked me to take a photo of him and Mwezi so he could send it to his wife and children," I say. "But then the funniest thing happened."

"Tell us!" Joon says.

"While the pilot and Mwezi were posing for the photo, the pilot's pants fell off! So in my photo, he is in his underwear!"

Leopold laughs so hard he snorts. "I'm not sure your story is true, Jelly, but it sure is funny," he says.

Joon is a better audience because she believes all my stories. "Weren't the other passengers nervous?" she asks. "I'd be nervous if I was sitting next to a lioness. Even if she was as well behaved as Mwezi."

"I was the one sitting next to her. There was only one passenger on the airplane who objected. An older man. It was because he had a severe cat allergy. He sneezed the whole way home," I say.

45

"*If*...and only *if* your story is true," Leopold says, "it must have been a very long flight from Africa to Canada. So what did Mwezi do during all that time?"

Leopold is trying to spoil my fun. But I won't let him. Besides, Leopold is no match for me and my imagination!

"You're right," I tell Leopold. "It was a long flight. In fact, it was two flights. First we had to fly from Kilimanjaro to Amsterdam. Then there was a six-hour layover before the flight to Montreal."

Joon puts her hands on her waist and looks Leopold in the eye. "Jelly wouldn't know all that if this was a made-up story."

"Maybe," Leopold says.

Maybe is progress. That inspires me to continue my story. "The flight from Kilimanjaro to Amsterdam took over

46

ten hours. But Mwezi spent most of that time sleeping. Lions love to sleep. It's another thing they have in common with house cats. Of course, I brought Mwezi's pajamas for her to wear, and I made her floss her teeth."

"Mwezi wears pajamas?" Joon sounds surprised.

"Only when she's traveling," I say. "They're blue flannel. She didn't like the pink ones."

Leopold raises his palm in the air. "Wait a second! Are you saying Mwezi speaks English?"

Leopold's question makes me realize that perhaps I have gone too far with my story. So I laugh—as hard as I can. "You're so funny, Leopold!" Every kid I ever met likes to hear that he or she is funny. "I wasn't saying Mwezi speaks English. But Mwezi and I communicate without words. She hissed when we were at the store and I showed her the pink pajamas. She roared when she saw the blue ones."

"What did you and Mwezi do during the layover in Amsterdam?" Joon asks.

"That was my favorite part of the trip," I tell her. "We took the train from the Schiphol airport"—my parents visited Amsterdam last year, so I know the name of the airport—"to downtown Amsterdam. Mwezi wanted to see a windmill."

Leopold raises his hand again. "How did Mwezi tell you *that*?" he asks.

"At the Schiphol airport, Mwezi kept looking at a poster with a windmill on it. That's how I knew she wanted to see a windmill."

"How did she behave on the flight to Montreal?" Joon asks.

"That was no problem at all. We watched movies the whole time."

"What movies?" Leopold asks.

How can one person think of so many questions? Maybe that's what makes Leopold a good reporter for his school newspaper. "*The Lion King*, of course. It's Mwezi's favorite. We watched it three times."

"I thought you said you watched *movies*. Not just one movie three times!" Leopold says.

I am trying to come up with an answer when Hilda and Ms. Jessup come running toward us. "A little boy said he saw a lion loose in our rescue center!" Ms. Jessup shouts. "We think he was just making up a story—you know how kids are—but we've come to check on Mwezi all the same."

Ms. Jessup and Hilda press their faces up against the wire of the enclosure.

"I don't see her. Do you?" Hilda says to Ms. Jessup.

"No, I don't see her either!" Ms. Jessup sounds worried.

Joon taps on Ms. Jessup's elbow. "Mwezi was lying in the sun before," Joon says. "We saw her."

"Why don't you ask your new part-time lion trainer to call her?" Leopold says.

Ms. Jessup raises her eyebrows. "New part-time lion trainer? What in the world are you talking about?"

Now Leopold and Joon will know that I've been making up stories!

Except that at this very moment, we have a bigger problem to deal with.

"Oh no! Look at the back of the enclosure!" Ms. Jessup says. "The gate is open. One of the animal keepers must have forgotten to close it. Mwezi *is* on the loose!"

Chapter Seven

"Code red. I repeat, code red. All visitors to the animal refuge center must report immediately to the main building. This is NOT A DRILL! All visitors, report IMMEDIATELY to the main building."

The announcement comes booming through the loudspeakers. *Code red* means a potentially dangerous animal has escaped its enclosure.

"What's going on?" I hear a woman ask.

Somewhere else, a dad is shushing his baby.

Several people are running down the path to the main building.

"A lion has esc—" Joon starts to shout, but when I squeeze her hand, she stops. It will only make things worse if people start to panic.

Joon spins around and glares at me. "You shouldn't have lied to us about being the new part-time lion trainer. I can't believe I fell for another one of your stories!" she says.

Leopold shakes his head. "I didn't believe her. Not for a second."

"Look," I tell them. "I'm really, really, super sorry. Believe me. I can explain more later. Right now I have to help find Mwezi!"

I do not realize that Ms. Jessup is standing behind me until she taps on my shoulder. "Angelica, you will not be helping to get Mwezi back. You and your friends are to report to the main building along with all the other visitors. Now!"

I can tell from Ms. Jessup's tone that there is no arguing with her.

Hilda is standing near the door to the main building, directing people inside.

"Can we get into our cars and go home?" a woman asks her.

"Absolutely not," Hilda says. "You'll have to wait inside until we can secure the perimeter."

"Has there been some kind of crime?" a man asks.

"There has not been a crime. But I'm afraid I can't provide any more details at the moment," Hilda tells him.

Ms. Jessup is huddled with two of the keepers who feed the animals. Though I cannot hear what they are saying, I know they must be coming up with a search plan.

The keepers scatter in different directions, and Ms. Jessup comes inside to address the crowd. The room goes quiet. Ms. Jessup clears her throat.

"I don't want anyone to panic, but the news I am about to share is rather disturbing. One of our rescue animals, the lioness Mwezi, has escaped from her enclosure. We have no reason to believe Mwezi is dangerous—in all the time she has lived in captivity, Mwezi has never hurt a human being—but as a precaution, we are asking all of you to stay inside here until the situation is under control. You can get drinks and donuts at the cafeteria—for no charge, of course," she says.

Leopold nudges me. "That's good news about the donuts."

Ms. Jessup does a head count of all the people gathered in the main building. "Thirty-one, thirty-two...hmm. According to our ticket-sales records, two people are missing." She takes her radio out of her pocket. "We need to locate them immediately and get them here."

Just as Ms. Jessup is about to speak into the radio, a woman in a flowery dress raises her hand. "I think I know who's missing. I saw an elderly couple by the beaver dam. The woman was in a wheelchair. They're not here."

"A wheelchair?" Ms. Jessup says. "Are you sure? Because this building is not wheelchair accessible." Ms. Jessup wipes her forehead. She lowers her voice as she speaks into the radio, but I'm close enough to hear her. "Two individuals are unaccounted for. I have reason to believe it's an elderly couple, and the woman is wheelchair bound. We need to locate the pair immediately—and deal with the wheelchair situation."

"I can help!" I call out.

"How can you help, Angelica?" Ms. Jessup asks.

"I can build a wheelchair ramp!" I say.

"That's not all Angelica can do!" Joon says. "She knows a trick for getting Mwezi to come over to her."

Ms. Jessup sighs. "I don't have time

right now for any more of Angelica's stories."

I'm glad Ms. Jessup did not use the word *lies*. I would not want everyone here thinking I am a liar. I see myself more as a storyteller who sometimes gets swept away by my own stories.

Joon has something else to say. "You don't understand, Ms. Jessup. This isn't a story. I've seen Jelly get Mwezi to come over. I swear I have!"

Ms. Jessup looks from Joon to me, then back at Joon and back at me. "Well then," Ms. Jessup says, "follow me, Angelica. When big cats like Mwezi get out of their enclosures, it's important to keep them calm. If what Joon is saying is true, I may be able to use your help with Mwezi. But you need to follow my instructions to the letter at all times."

I do not mention to Ms. Jessup what I am thinking, which is that I hope the elderly couple has not met Mwezi. Mwezi may have never attacked a person while she was living in her enclosure, but I know enough about lions to know that once they get back out in the wild, their behavior can change.

"Oh, thank goodness," Ms. Jessup says, pointing straight ahead when we get outside. At first I think she has spotted Mwezi. But when I look at where she is pointing, I see an elderly couple coming toward us. The man is pushing a wheelchair with a woman in it.

"We just heard the announcement," the man calls to Ms. Jessup. "But I don't know how I'm going to get my wife inside the main building. There is no wheelchair access. All public buildings should have wheelchair access."

"I can help!" I call out to the couple.

"You can?" the woman says. "How wonderful!"

"What are you going to do?" her husband asks.

"We...uh..." I usually like to have some time to come up with a solution. But there is no time today. Not if I want to help Ms. Jessup and her team find Mwezi!

My eyes land on the bench I just fixed. On the grass near the bench is the overturned sign Hilda left there.

"We can use that piece of plywood for a ramp!"

The woman in the wheelchair claps. "What's your name, dear?" she asks me.

"Angelica," I tell her. "But you can call me Jelly."

Chapter Eight

"Hurry! Hurry!" the elderly man says as Ms. Jessup and I drag the piece of plywood to the main building. "Code red means the situation is dire!"

But there is no sign of Mwezi.

The plywood is not the perfect size, but it will do. I help the man maneuver the wheelchair onto the plywood ramp and into the building.

The old man and his wife want to shake my hand, but I explain there isn't time. "I need to help Ms. Jessup find Mwezi," I tell them.

"Are you sure that's safe?" the woman asks.

"You're just a child," her husband says.

Joon has been listening in on the conversation. "Jelly may be a child. And even if she isn't the new part-time lion trainer, she *is* good with lions."

"Well, good luck, dear," the old woman says, blowing me a kiss. "Promise to be careful out there!"

Ms. Jessup announces that except for the search party, everyone must remain inside the main building. For security reasons, the door must be locked.

One of the keepers heads east to look for Mwezi. The other keeper heads west.

Ms. Jessup and I walk down the main pathway that leads through the middle of the animal property, past Mwezi's enclosure. She explains that sometimes animals who have escaped will return to their enclosures because that is where they feel most comfortable.

A snowy owl watches us from a high branch in its enclosure. Perhaps this owl knows where Mwezi went. If only animals could talk!

Mwezi is not in her enclosure. We look for her in the bushes and in the tall grasses by the marsh. We look for her underneath two stone bridges.

Ms. Jessup uses her radio to contact the keepers who are searching for Mwezi. But they have no news.

"I wish I knew what was going on in Mwezi's head," Ms. Jessup mutters.

"We could try imagining to be her," I say.

"Imagining being a lion?" Ms. Jessup says. "I don't think that's possible."

"When it comes to using your imagination," I say, "anything is possible. I've imagined being a princess and a part-time lion trainer."

Though Ms. Jessop nods, I get the feeling her mind is elsewhere.

So in the same way that I imagined all the tricks I would teach Mwezi if I were a part-time lion trainer, and all the adventures Mwezi and I might have had if we were together on an airplane, I try imagining what it would feel like to be Mwezi.

If I were Mwezi and I'd been living for many years at an animal rescue center with people peering at me all day long, I think I'd feel excited if I escaped from my enclosure.

I'd want to explore all the places I could never see from inside my enclosure.

I think I might also feel afraid. That would make me want to hide.

And I think that after so many years of having people peer at *me*, well, I'd want to peer at *them*!

So where would I go to explore, hide and watch people?

I'd want to explore as much of the area as possible. I'd probably head for the fence along the edge of the property and follow the path beside it.

I would hide in secret places. Or in places where there was camouflage. Places that were yellowish-colored like me.

I could watch people from the lookout tower.

The lookout tower is near the fence. I suggest to Ms. Jessup that we go there first. We look for paw prints on the ground, but we don't see any. When we get to the tower, Mwezi is not there.

We take the stairs to the top of the tower. That way we'll get a view of the entire area.

"What's yellow at this animal refuge center?" I ask Ms. Jessup as we climb the stairs.

"Why?" she says.

"Maybe Mwezi is looking for a place where she will be camouflaged."

When we reach the top of tower, we look out in every direction. I spot one of the keepers. Ms. Jessup spots the other. But neither of us spots Mwezi.

"The only place on the property that's yellow," Ms. Jessup says, "is the field of sunflowers."

So we head over to the field, but Mwezi is not there either.

Suddenly, we hear loud honking coming from a car in the parking lot in front of the center. The honking is nonstop.

Ms. Jessup throws her hands up into the air. "That honking could frighten Mwezi. As I explained before, it's very important that Mwezi stays calm. We've got to get to the parking lot and tell whoever it is to stop!"

When we reach the parking lot, it's easy to tell which car the honking is coming from.

There's a yellow convertible parked on a hill at the edge of the lot.

It's the same shade of yellow as Mwezi's coat.

That yellow convertible would be good for exploring, hiding and watching.

"Look!" I say to Ms. Jessup. I point to the back seat of the convertible.

Mwezi's in it!

And that's not all. Mwezi is so big that even from the back seat, she can reach the steering wheel. Not only can she reach it, but she can also chew on it! And with every chew, Mwezi hits the horn. Now we know who's been honking!

Chapter Nine

"Thank goodness we've found Mwezi!" Ms. Jessup says. "But how are we ever going to get her out of that convertible?"

"Can I try blowing to get her attention?" I ask Ms. Jessup.

"Go ahead," she says.

But when I try blowing to get Mwezi to come over, she does not budge.

"We can offer her some food," Ms. Jessup suggests. "I brought along a frozen mouse. Frozen mice are one of Mwezi's favorite treats."

But Mwezi ignores the frozen mouse.

"I have something she might like," I tell Ms. Jessup. I reach into my pocket for the bit of leftover meatball that I have wrapped in a napkin. I wave the piece of meatball at Mwezi, but she still won't budge.

Ms. Jessup thinks we should phone the fire department. "I was confident we could handle this emergency on our own, but now I think we may need extra help."

"Let me try something first," I say.

"What do you have in mind?" Ms. Jessup asks.

"I want to jack up the convertible," I say.

"How will that help?" Ms. Jessup asks.

"You'll see. But first I need a car jack."

There is a jack in Ms. Jessup's car, though she has never used it. She goes to get the jack from her trunk. "Bring the spare tire too," I call after her.

"How will that help?" she asks.

"You'll see."

When she comes back I slip the spare tire underneath the trunk of the car. If something goes wrong, the car will not crush me. Then I feel underneath the car for the right place to set up the jack.

"Who taught you how to do that?" Ms. Jessup sounds impressed.

"My parents."

Ms. Jessup watches as I crank the jack.

Slowly the back of the convertible begins to rise.

Mwezi roars as she tumbles from the back seat to the front seat.

Ms. Jessup must have radioed the two keepers, because they come running to the parking lot. One has a dart gun. When Mwezi sees the gun, she lets out another terrible roar.

"Put that gun away!" I tell the keeper. "You are upsetting Mwezi."

The keeper ignores me. He turns to Ms. Jessup. "We need to get Mwezi back in her enclosure as soon as possible. The tranquilizer in the dart gun will calm Mwezi down so we can move her."

Ms. Jessup rubs her forehead. Mwezi has not stopped roaring. The sound is even louder than when Mwezi was honking the car horn.

"Ms. Jessup! Don't you see that the dart gun is making Mwezi more upset? Maybe it reminds her of the day her leg was caught in the trap!"

"Jelly could be right," Ms. Jessup says. Then she turns to the worker and asks him to put away the dart gun.

Mwezi lets out another roar, but then she stops.

"There must be another way to calm Mwezi and get her back to her enclosure," Ms. Jessup says.

Just then there is a rattling at the gate that leads to the parking lot. It's Joon.

"What are you doing here?" one of the keepers asks her.

"I told you all to stay in the main building—and to keep the door locked!" Ms. Jessup sounds like she's about to lose her cool.

"I couldn't wait inside any longer," Joon says. "I was worried about Jelly. She's my best friend."

"I am?" I say to Joon. "Does that mean you've forgiven me?"

Ms. Jessup rubs her forehead. "Girls," she says, "now isn't the time to discuss the state of your friendship. We are trying to find a way to calm Mwezi down so we can get her back in her enclosure."

Joon points at me. "Jelly can calm anybody down," she says, "even a lioness! All she has to do is tell one of her stories."

Which is how I end up sitting on the pavement in the parking lot, telling Mwezi the story of how I got my start as a part-time lion trainer.

"Ms. Jessup asked me to carry a chair to the conference room," I tell Mwezi. "On the way, I met a boy named Leopold. When he asked me if I was a lion trainer, I started to say no, but then I changed my mind."

Mwezi crouches down on her front legs. She is getting into my story.

A lot of my stories start out with something true, but then my imagination takes over.

"I was training a lioness when the porcupine living in the next enclosure escaped," I say.

Mwezi licks her front paws. Lions do not like porcupines. If a lion attacks a porcupine, the porcupine's quills can get stuck in the lion's mouth. Sometimes the quills get stuck there forever!

"The porcupine crawled under a fence and into the lioness's enclosure. It was nighttime, but as you know, the lioness could see in the dark, like all cats. She wasn't planning to eat the porcupine. (The lioness had had two helpings of meatballs for her supper.) All the lioness wanted to do was tell that porcupine to go home.

"But the porcupine panicked. He lowered his back, which is what porcupines do when they are upset. The lioness roared. Her mouth was open, and five porcupine quills got in!

"I brought the lioness to the dentist. Luckily, the dentist had a big chair. The dentist removed all the quills, but the lioness was still angry with that porcupine. She wanted the porcupine to pay the dentist bill.

"So on the way home from the dentist's office, the lioness asked me whether we could stop in at the porcupine's enclosure.

"Of course I said yes. No one argues with a lioness."

Mwezi roars at that part of the story.

"What happened next?" Ms. Jessup asks.

"A snowy owl was flying overhead. Owls are one of the few animals that know how to hunt for porcupines. That snowy owl was just about to swoop down on the porcupine when—"

"Doesn't Jelly tell the best stories?" Joon asks.

"Shhh, don't interrupt," Ms. Jessup tells her.

"—when the lioness roared. The snowy owl flew off into the night. And the porcupine paid the dentist bill."

Ms. Jessup, Joon and the two keepers clap when I reach the end of the story.

Mwezi yawns. At first I worry she didn't enjoy my story. But then Ms. Jessup raises one finger in the air and says, "Like all cats, lions yawn when they are relaxed. I think that now, thanks to you, Jelly, Mwezi is ready to let us lead her back to her enclosure."

Chapter Ten

I am sitting with Joon and Leopold on the bench outside Mwezi's enclosure. "Make Mwezi come over!" Joon says.

Today when I blow on the bars of the enclosure, Mwezi's ears turn up, and she comes bounding over.

"You really are good with lions," Leopold says. "But you never put your head in Mwezi's mouth, did you?"

"Okay, I admit it. I didn't. I'm sorry I tried to fool you two. Sometimes when I tell a story, I get carried away by my own imagination."

"Did I hear someone say *imagination?*"

It is Ms. Jessup. She and Hilda are carrying the new bench.

"This bench is made of fiberglass," Hilda says. "It should last thirty years."

The three of us get up to help Ms. Jessup and Hilda. They want to put the new bench next to the old one.

"Did you see the plaque?" Hilda asks.

There is a bronze plaque on the new bench. Engraved on the plaque are the words *In Thanks to Jelly, Part-time Lion Trainer*.

I am so happy that for once I have no words.

With Thanks to Jelly

Part-Time
Lion Trainer

Ms. Jessup claps my shoulder. "We put the plaque on the bench as a way to thank you for helping us get Mwezi back in her enclosure."

"Does that mean Jelly really is a part-time lion trainer?" Joon asks.

Ms. Jessup looks me in the eye. "As a matter of fact, I want to offer you a volunteer position, Jelly. Your official title will be part-time lion trainer, though your duties will be filling the animals' bowls with water and helping Hilda with repairs."

"That sounds amazing," I tell Ms. Jessup.

"Now that that's settled," Joon says, "do you think you can find a job for me too? Maybe you could put me in charge of collecting people's suggestions for improving this place—like selling cotton candy in the cafeteria and having a designated area where the animals can come to look at the people!"

"That would make a great article for my school newspaper," Leopold says.

He and I test the new bench. He stretches his legs out in front of him and sighs. "Jelly," he says, "why don't you tell us another story?"

Mwezi roars.

I think that means she is in the mood for another story too.

MONIQUE POLAK has written many novels for young adults, including her historical novel *What World is Left*, which won the 2009 Quebec Writers' Federation Prize for Children's and Young Adult Literature. When not writing award-winning books, Monique teaches English and humanities at Marianopolis College in Montreal, Quebec. She is also an active freelance journalist. For more information, visit moniquepolak.com.